MRS. WATSON WANTS YOUR TEETH

STORY BY

Alison McGhee

PICTURES BY

Harry Bliss

Voyager Books
Harcourt, Inc.
Orlando   Austin   New York   San Diego   London

Requests for permission to make copies of any part of the work
should be submitted online at www.harcourt.com/contact
or mailed to the following address: Permissions Department,
Harcourt, Inc., 6277 Sea Harbor Drive, Orlando, Florida 32887-6777.

www.HarcourtBooks.com

First Voyager Books edition 2008

Voyager Books is a trademark of Harcourt, Inc., registered in the
United States of America and/or other jurisdictions.

The Library of Congress has cataloged the hardcover edition as follows:
McGhee, Alison, 1960–
Mrs. Watson wants your teeth/by Alison McGhee; pictures by Harry Bliss.
p. cm.
Summary: A first grader is frightened on her first day of school
after hearing a rumor that her teacher is a 300-year-old
alien with a purple tongue who steals baby teeth from her students.
[1. Schools—Fiction. 2. First day of school—Fiction.
3. Teachers—Fiction. 4. Teeth—Fiction.]
I. Bliss, Harry, 1964– ill. II. Title.
PZ7.M4784675Mr 2004
[E]—dc22   2003021267
ISBN 978-0-15-204931-7
ISBN 987-0-15-206348-1 pb

A C E G H F D B

The pictures in this book were done in black ink
and watercolor on Arches 90 lb. watercolor paper.
The display lettering was created by Jane Dill.
The text type was hand-lettered by Paul Colin.
Color separations by Bright Arts Ltd., Hong Kong
Manufactured by South China Printing Company, Ltd., China
Production supervision by Christine Witnik
Designed by Suzanne Fridley and Scott Piehl

For Min O'Brien
—A. M.

For my hilarious, toothless,
hockey-playing son, Alex
—H. B.

I have a secret. . . .

First grade begins today, and I'm in BIG trouble.

It's a known fact that Mrs. Watson, the first-grade teacher, is a three-hundred-year-old alien who steals baby teeth from her students.

How do I know? A second grader told me.

My secret? I have a loose tooth! It's my first one.

It's so loose that every
time I take a bite, I expect
it to fall right out.

I miss my kindergarten teacher. She was the one who taught me how to tie my shoes.

I did it!

She let me bring stuffed animals to class.

And she did *not* have a "treat box" or a purple tongue.

PINK

AFTER SHARING...

I want to get a good look at Mrs. Watson's purple tongue ...

and those
earrings ...

and her "pearl"
necklace. . . .

At snack time, I look up. Guess who is right there?

It's going to be a long year—a long, silent, snackless, tooth-protecting year.

At recess, I look up. Guess who's right there?

BACK IN CLASS...

Does that boy know that Mrs. Watson is really a three-hundred-year-old alien with a purple tongue who needs earthling baby teeth in order to survive? I have to warn him!

Mrs. Watson comes toward *me* with the treat box!

And that's when it happens. . . .

I get a good look at Mrs. Watson's pearl necklace...

and her earrings...

and I get an extra good look at the treat box!

AFTER SCHOOL...